SINS OF THE SON

First Published in Great Britain 2021 by Mirador Publishing

First edition: 2021

Any reference to real names and places are purely fictional and are constructs of the author. Any offence the references produce is unintentional and in no way reflects the reality of any locations or people involved.

ISBN: 978-1-914965-16-6

Mirador Publishing
10 Greenbrook Terrace
Taunton
Somerset
UK
TA1 1UT